HOW THE CRITTERS CREATED TEXAS

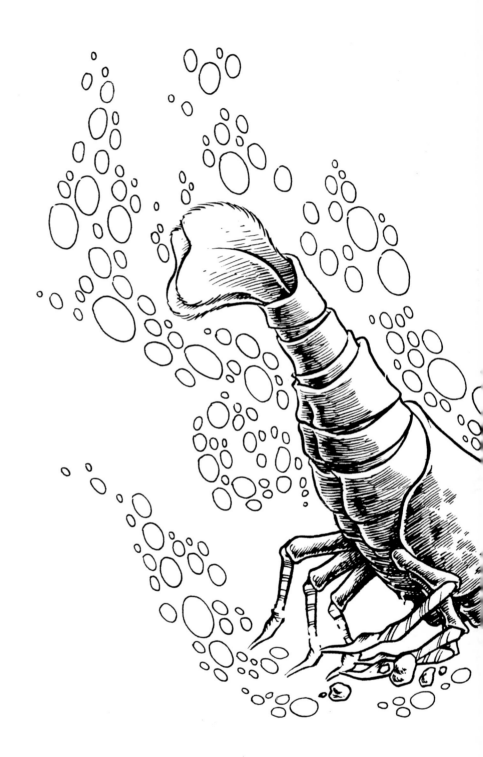

How the Critters Created Texas

by Francis Edward Abernethy

illustrated by Ben Sargent

Ellen C. Temple · Publisher / Austin Texas

Library of Congress Cataloging in Publication Data

Abernethy, Francis Edward.
  How the critters created Texas.

   1. Alibamu Indians—Legends. 2. Koasati Indians—
Legends. 3. Indians of North America—Texas—Legends.
4. Legends—Texas. I. Sargent, Ben, 1948–
II. Title.
E99.A4A23 1982   398.2′08997   82-80440
ISBN 0-936650-01-X (pbk.)

ISBN 0-936650-01-X
LC 82-80440
Design/Eje Wray
Typesetting/G&S Typesetters

Preface

The Alabama and Coushatta Indians tell a story that they came out of a hole in the ground on opposite sides of a tree in what is now the state of Alabama. The two tribes hunted and fished together for many generations before the white man came. Then, pushed ahead by a wave of American settlers, they made their long journey to a new hunting ground in East Texas. Many of the Alabama-Coushatta Indians still live in East Texas on their own reservation in Polk County.

When Howard Martin was a young man living in Polk County in the 1930's, he went to school with the Alabama-Coushatta Indians. He played with them and visited in their homes, and they told him the stories their parents and grandparents had told them. Howard wrote the stories down and later published them in a Texas Folklore Society book. (Martin, Howard N., <u>Myths and Folktales of the Alabama-Coushata Indians of Texas</u>. Austin, Texas: Encino Press, 1977.)

As an East Texan and a folklorist, I was interested in these Indian folktales, and as a parent I was, by frequent request, a story teller. My children liked to hear stories, so I told them some of the Alabama-Coushatta tales. The creation story with its raft of animals was a favorite. In my mind's eye, the little animals, grumping around or playing in the mud, were acting like people, and that is how I saw them when I eventually wrote the story. My children liked it, and on one occasion the story was presented as a play by grade-school children.

This old Indian folktale of creation has come a long way since its first telling, but it is still a good story. The old ones would recognize it and understand the human quality of the animals perhaps better than we. And we moderns, who are always probing into the beginnings of things, can appreciate its playful fancy. The story has given pleasure to many people over a long period of time. We hope it still does.

Francis Edward Abernethy
Nacogdoches, Texas

In the beginning the hills and plains of Texas were without form and were void, and water covered the face of the deep. The sky was blue and the sea was blue and that is all that there was—except for one big cypress-log raft that floated right in the middle of the sea, somewhere between Austin and Lampasas.

The raft had been floating since the beginning of time, and the creatures that wandered about on the raft had been there as long as the raft had. They had been there so long that they had gotten awful tired of the robin's-egg blue sky and beautiful blue-green sea, and they were

tired of the fine cypress-log raft, and Fox was
tired of playing dominoes with Wolf, and Jaybird
was tired of talking to 'Possum. They never got
hungry and they never had to work, and they
were bored and dissatisfied, and all they did
was gripe and whine.

"I'm sure tired of this old raft," whined Armadillo. "I wish I had a rotten log to root around in. I'd eat a grub worm."

"Grub worm! Yetch!" gagged Javelina. "I wish I had this whole raft growing with prickly pear."

"Yea, gee, really! Me, too!" squeaked Woodrat. "I wish I had a bunch of prickly pear to burrow up in."

"I wouldn't burrow up in it, silly; I'd eat it," said Javelina, popping his teeth snappishly.

Snake, who talked through her nose in a long thin little voice, said, "Wish, wish, wish! That's all we do around here. Nothing fun ever happens and I'm b-o-a-r-d—bored. And I'm getting mighty tired of all these animals and all this hair and feathers and fur." And she snuck off in a snakish snit and curled herself in a pile and sulked.

One evening Fox called them all together.
"There must be something better," he said,
"than spending eternity floating on a raft."

Everybody clapped and whistled in agreement.
"I think," he continued, "that we ought to find
some land." More cheers. "Now who will
volunteer to go in search of land?"

There was a lot of mumbling and looking for excuses.

Owl said, "Onliest time I could go is at night, so I guess that cuts me out."

"I'd go but I gotta finish this web by Saturday," said Spider.

Turkey Hen quickly walked to the edge of the raft and began thoughtfully studying the water, first with one eye then the other, as if she had something real important to do.

Terrapin pulled in his head and clamped down on his shell like nobody was at home.

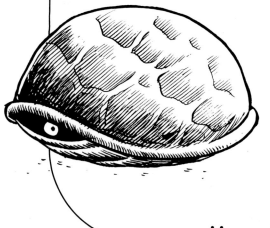

Hummingbird hummed.

Finally Muskrat stood up and said, "I'm probably the best swimmer here, so I shall swim out to see if I can find some land."

Muskrat left early the next morning but at nightfall he was back, exhausted. "I swam a great circle around the raft," he said, "but I couldn't find anything that looked like land."

That evening they gathered again and Crow said, "I'm probably the best flyer here, so I shall fly up to see if I can find some land."

Crow left early the next morning but at nightfall he was back, exhausted. "I flew a great circle around the raft," he said, "but I couldn't find anything that looked like land."

That evening they gathered again, and Fox said, "If the land is not out or up, it must be down. Now who will volunteer to go down in search of land?"

Crawfish said, "I'm probably the best diver here, so I shall dive down and see if I can find land."

Crawfish left early the next morning. By the middle of the afternoon, she was back with a piece of land in her claw.

Everybody cheered and hollered and they had
a parade, carrying Crawfish around on their
shoulders. Then they got to wondering what
good land would do them as long as it was
down there and they were up here. At first they

wanted Crawfish to bring it up so that they could plaster the raft with it. Then they decided that Crawfish could just build a big crawfish chimney up from the bottom of the sea.

Crawfish argued a while because she knew
what a job it was going to be, but everybody
talked so loud at her that she went on back
down and began building her chimney.

Crawfish worked on her chimney almost a week, scraping up balls of mud with her tail and patting them in place with her claws. Finally she got it up to sea level, but to make sure that she had plenty she kept adding mud until the top of the chimney spilled out in a great broad plain as far as the eye could see.

All the animals jumped off the raft and began
wading around in the mud and rolling in it and
making mudpies and laughing and giggling at
each other's tracks. They played all that day and
then got up early the next morning to play some

more. Late that afternoon when they were getting a little tired, Banty Hen said, "All this mud is better than that raft, but it sure is flat. It looks like Lubbock County to me."

Everbody got to looking around, and sure
enough, it did look like the flat West Texas
plains.

    "Looks great to me," barked Prairie Dog.

    "Me, too," said Coyote. "I like open space
to howl in."

    "Well, I don't particularly like it," said
Raccoon. "It ought to look more like East Texas,
with creeks and pine trees and red dirt and
stuff."

Panther, who wasn't very sociable anyhow, said he always thought the world ought to look like big rocky mountains with bear grass and cactus growing everywhere, where there was some privacy.

Well, they all started arguing about how the world—or at least, Texas—ought to be decorated. Some wanted pine and post oak, some wanted mesquite—some wanted sandy land to play in, some wanted old black gumbo—a lot of water or a little—sagebrush or yaupon. Before long they were back sitting on the edge of the raft, still arguing, dangling their feet in the mud, watching Badger and Prairie Dog trying to figure out where to dig their holes.

Buzzard drooped around and thought awhile.
Then he said, "Don't you all worry. I'll make it
look like Texas!"

　　So he flew out in ever widening circles,
flapping his big wings and soaring. Every time

he flapped down he made a valley, and when he flapped up he made a mountain. Sometimes he just soared and rested and made flat meadows and prairies. Finally he flew one last pass from north to south and dragged his wing tips. On the west he cut the Rio Grande and the Pecos Rivers. On the east he cut the Neches and the Sabine.

And through the middle he dragged his toes and scratched out the Colorado and the Brazos.

Buzzard then lit on the top of Enchanted Rock
and looked at all that he had done. He could see
all the way from the Big Bend to the Big Thicket
and from the Panhandle to the Valley, and he
could see all his friends running up and down

the hills and mountains and poking around the
arroyos and creek banks. Some of them had
already started setting out cedar trees and
scattering poke salad seeds.

So Buzzard pulled his head in between his shoulders, smiled a satisfied smile, and took a nap

because he could tell that it was good!

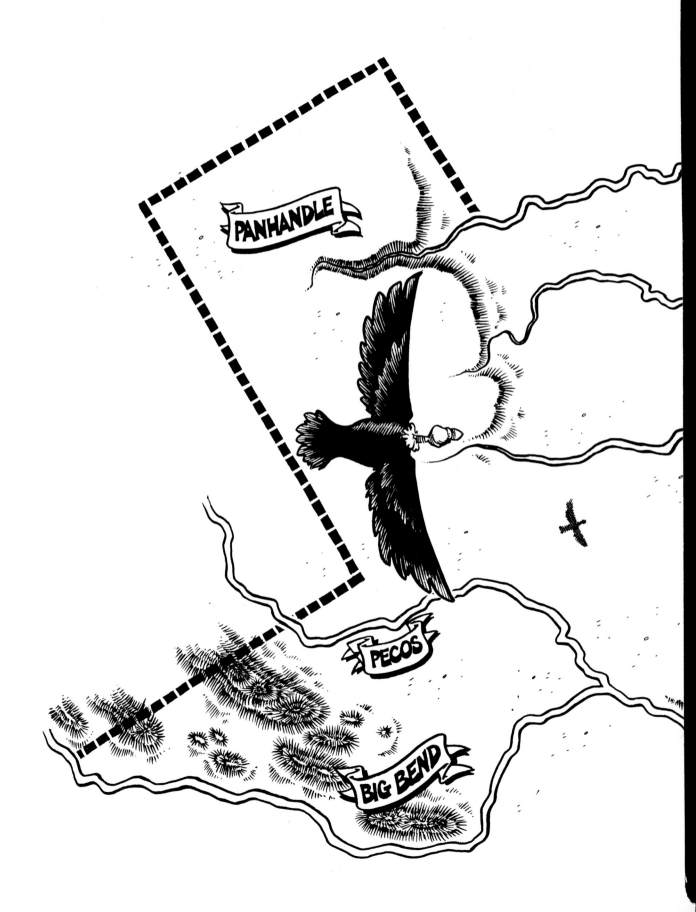

Ben Sargent, editorial cartoonist for the Austin American-Statesman, is the winner of the 1982 Pulitzer Prize for editorial cartooning. Born in Amarillo, Texas, of a newspaper family, Sargent received his bachelor of journalism degree from the University of Texas at Austin in 1970. He worked as a reporter for five years, mainly covering the State Capitol for the Corpus Christi Caller-Times, Long News Service, the Austin American-Statesman, and United Press International. He started drawing editorial cartoons for the Austin American-Statesman in 1974 and is now distributed nationally by United Feature Syndicate. Author of Texas Statehood Blues, published by Texas Monthly Press in 1980, Sargent has illustrated several other books. He, his wife and 2 year old daughter live in Austin, Texas.

Francis Edward Abernethy is Professor of English at Stephen F. Austin State University and the executive secretary and editor of the Texas Folklore Society. Dr. Abernethy attended Stephen F. Austin State University, the University of Neuchatel (Switzerland) and Louisiana State University, where he received his doctorate in Renaissance literature. He has taught at Louisiana State University, Lamar State University, and Stephen F. Austin State University. He is the editor of Tales from the Big Thicket and Built in Texas, Legendary Ladies of Texas, and five other volumes for the Texas Folklore Society. He has published poetry and short stories and has lectured widely, both popularly and academically. He plays the bass fiddle in the East Texas String ensemble and lives in Nacogdoches, East Texas. He has a wife and five children and is undescribably sophisticated, handsome and witty.